A Child's Christmas in Wales

Dylan Thomas

Praise for *A Child's Christmas in Wales* . . .

'Dylan Thomas's homage to the Christmases of
his boyhood, when the snow was thicker and whiter,
when everything about Christmas was better than
it is now . . . It's the sheer acrobatic brilliance
of the language here that we love the most.
This is the most delicious read-aloud for having
words trip off the tongue'
Elizabeth Blumele, Publisher's Weekly

'For those who have never read this delightful story here is a chance to be enchanted by its simplicity and style . . . There is a magical quality about this story which captures a child's feelings at Christmas. It is full of fun and memories'

Celtic Press

This illustrated edition first published in Great Britain
in 2014 by Orion Children's Books
This paperback edition first published in Great Britain in 2016
by Hodder and Stoughton

3 5 7 9 10 8 6 4 2

A CIP catalogue record for this book
is available from the British Library.

Hardback ISBN 978 1 4440 1346 7
Paperback ISBN 978 1 4440 1543 0

Printed in China

The paper and board used in this book are from well-managed forests
and other responsible sources.

Orion Children's Books
An imprint of
Hachette Children's Group
Part of Hodder and Stoughton
Carmelite House
50 Victoria Embankment
London EC4Y 0DZ

An Hachette UK Company
www.hachette.co.uk
www.hachettechildrens.co.uk

A Child's Christmas in Wales

Dylan Thomas

Illustrated by
Peter Bailey

Orion
Children's Books

ne Christmas was so much like
   another, in those years around
the sea-town corner now and out of all sound
   except the distant speaking of the voices
   I sometimes hear a moment before sleep,
that I can never remember whether it snowed
for six days and six nights when I was twelve
   or whether it snowed for twelve days and
        twelve nights when I was six.

All the Christmases roll down toward
the two-tongued sea, like a cold and
headlong moon bundling down the sky that was
our street; and they stop at the rim of the ice-
edged, fish-freezing waves, and I plunge
my hands in the snow and bring out
whatever I can find.

In goes my hand into that wool-white bell-
tongued ball of holidays resting at the
rim of the carol-singing sea, and out come
Mrs Prothero and the firemen.

It was on the afternoon of the day of Christmas Eve, and I was in Mrs Prothero's garden, waiting for cats, with her son Jim. It was snowing. It was always snowing at Christmas. December, in my memory, was as white as Lapland, though there were no reindeers. But there were cats.

Patient, cold and callous, our hands wrapped in socks, we waited to snowball the cats. Sleek and long as jaguars and horrible-whiskered, spitting and snarling, they would slink and sidle over the white back-garden walls, and the lynx-eyed hunters, Jim and I, fur-capped and moccasined trappers from Hudson Bay, off Mumbles Road, would hurl our deadly snowballs at the green of their eyes.

The wise cats never appeared.

We were so still, Eskimo-footed arctic marksmen in the muffling silence of the eternal snows — eternal, ever since Wednesday — that we never heard Mrs Prothero's first cry from her igloo at the bottom of the garden. Or, if we heard it at all, it was, to us, like the far-off challenge of our enemy and prey, the neighbour's polar cat.

ut soon the voice grew louder.

'Fire!' cried Mrs Prothero,
and she beat the dinner-gong.

nd we ran down the garden, with the snowballs in our arms, toward the house; and smoke, indeed, was pouring out of the dining-room, and the gong was bombilating, and Mrs Prothero was announcing ruin like a town crier in Pompeii.

This was better than all the cats in Wales standing on the wall in a row. We bounded into the house, laden with snowballs, and stopped at the open door of the smoke-filled room.

Something was burning all right; perhaps it was Mr Prothero, who always slept there after midday dinner with a newspaper over his face. But he was standing in the middle of the room, saying, 'A fine Christmas!' and smacking at the smoke with a slipper.

'Call the fire brigade,' cried Mrs Prothero as she beat the gong.

'They won't be there,' said Mr Prothero, 'it's Christmas.'

There was no fire to be seen, only clouds of smoke and Mr Prothero standing in the middle of them, waving his slipper as though he were conducting.

'Do something,' he said.

And we threw all our snowballs into the
smoke – I think we missed
Mr Prothero – and ran out of the house
to the telephone box.

'Let's call the police as well,' Jim said.

'And the ambulance.'

'And Ernie Jenkins, he likes fires.'

But we only called the fire brigade, and soon the fire engine came and three tall men in helmets brought a hose into the house and Mr Prothero got out just in time before they turned it on.

Nobody could have had a noisier Christmas Eve. And when the firemen turned off the hose and were standing in the wet, smoky room, Jim's aunt, Miss Prothero, came downstairs and peered in at them.

Jim and I waited, very quietly, to hear what she would say to them. She said the right thing, always. She looked at the three tall firemen in their shining helmets, standing among the smoke and cinders and dissolving snowballs, and she said: 'Would you like anything to read?'

Years and years and years ago, when
I was a boy, when there were wolves
in Wales, and birds the colour of red-flannel
petticoats whisked past the harp-shaped hills,
when we sang and wallowed all night and day
in caves that smelt like Sunday afternoons in
damp front farmhouse parlours and we chased,
with the jawbones of deacons, the English
and the bears, before the motor-car, before the
wheel, before the duchess-faced horse, when we
rode the daft and happy hills bareback,
it snowed and it snowed.

ut here a small boy says: 'It snowed last year, too. I made a snowman and my brother knocked it down and I knocked my brother down and then we had tea.'

'But that was not the same snow,' I say.
'Our snow was not only shaken
from whitewash buckets down the sky, it came
shawling out of the ground and swam and
drifted out of the arms and hands and bodies
of the trees; snow grew overnight on the roofs
of the houses like a pure and grandfather moss,
minutely white-ivied the walls and settled on the
postman, opening the gate, like a dumb, numb
thunderstorm of white, torn Christmas cards.'

'ere there postmen then, too?'

'With sprinkling eyes and wind-cherried noses, on spread, frozen feet they crunched up to the doors and mittened on them manfully. But all that the children could hear was a ringing of bells.'

'You mean that the postman went rat-a-tat-tat and the doors rang?'

'I mean that the bells that the children could hear were inside them.'

'I only hear thunder sometimes, never bells.'

'There were church bells, too.'

'Inside them?'

No, no, no, in the bat-black, snow-white belfries, tugged by bishops and storks. And they rang their tidings over the bandaged town, over the frozen foam of the powder and ice-cream hills, over the crackling sea. It seemed that all the churches boomed for joy under my window; and the weathercocks crew for Christmas, on our fence.'

'Get back to the postmen.'

'They were just ordinary postmen, fond of walking and dogs and Christmas and the snow. They knocked on the doors with blue knuckles . . .'

'Ours has got a black knocker . . .'

'And then they stood on the white
Welcome mat in the little, drifted
porches and huffed and puffed, making ghosts
with their breath, and jogged from foot to foot
like small boys wanting to go out.'

'And then the Presents?'

'And then the Presents, after the
Christmas box. And the cold
postman, with a rose on his button-nose,
tingled down the tea-tray-slithered run of the
chilly glinting hill. He went in his ice-bound
boots like a man on fishmonger's slabs.
He wagged his bag like a frozen camel's hump,
dizzily turned the corner on one foot, and,
by God, he was gone.'

'Get back to the Presents.'

'There were the Useful Presents: engulfing mufflers of the old coach days, and mittens made for giant sloths; zebra scarfs of a substance like silky gum that could be tug-o'-warred down to the galoshes; blinding tam-o'-shanters like patchwork tea cosies and bunny-suited busbies and balaclavas for victims of head-shrinking tribes; from aunts who always wore wool next to the skin there were moustached and rasping vests that made you wonder why the aunts had any skin left at all; and once I had a little crocheted nose bag from an aunt now, alas, no longer whinnying with us. And pictureless books in which small boys, though warned with quotations not to, *would* skate on Farmer Giles' pond and did and drowned; and books that told me everything about the wasp, except why.'

'Go on to the Useless Presents.'

'Bags of moist and many-coloured jelly babies and a folded flag and a false nose and a tram-conductor's cap and a machine that punched tickets and rang a bell; never a catapult; once, by mistake that no one could explain, a little hatchet; and a celluloid duck that made, when you pressed it, a most unducklike sound, a mewing moo that an ambitious cat might make who wished to be a cow; and a painting book in which I could make the grass, the trees, the sea and the animals any colour I pleased, and still the dazzling sky-blue sheep are grazing in the red field under the rainbow-billed and pea-green birds.

'Hardboileds, toffee, fudge and allsorts, crunches, cracknels, humbugs, glaciers, marzipan, and butterwelsh for the Welsh. And troops of bright tin soldiers who, if they could not fight, could always run. And Snakes-and-Families and Happy Ladders. And Easy Hobbi-Games for Little Engineers, complete with instructions.

'Oh, easy for Leonardo! And a whistle to make the dogs bark to wake up the old man next door to make him beat on the wall with his stick to shake our picture off the wall.

36

'And a packet of cigarettes; you put one in your mouth and you stood at the corner of the street and you waited for hours, in vain, for an old lady to scold you for smoking a cigarette, and then with a smirk you ate it. And then it was breakfast under the balloons.'

'Were there Uncles like in our house?'

'There are always Uncles at Christmas.

'The same Uncles. And on Christmas mornings, with dog-disturbing whistle and sugar fags, I would scour the swatched town for the news of the little world, and find always a dead bird by the white Post Office or by the deserted swings;

perhaps a robin, all but one of his fires out.
Men and women wading or scooping back from
chapel, with taproom noses and wind-bussed
cheeks, all albinos, huddled their stiff black
jarring feathers against the irreligious snow.

'Mistletoe hung from the gas brackets
in all the front parlours;
there was sherry and
walnuts and bottled beer and crackers by the
dessertspoons; and cats in their fur-abouts
watched the fires; and the high-heaped fire spat,
all ready for the chestnuts and the mulling pokers.

'S ome few large men sat in the front
parlours, without their collars,
Uncles almost certainly, trying their new cigars,
holding them out judiciously at arms' length,
returning them to their mouths, coughing,
then holding them out again as though waiting
for the explosion;

And some few small Aunts, not wanted
in the kitchen, nor anywhere else
for that matter, sat on the very edges of their
chairs, poised and brittle, afraid to break,
like faded cups and saucers.'

Not many those mornings trod
the piling streets: an old man
always, fawn-bowlered, yellow-gloved and, at
this time of year, with spats of snow, would
take his constitutional to the white bowling
green and back, as he would take it wet or fine
on Christmas Day or Doomsday; sometimes
two hale young men, with big pipes blazing, no
overcoats and wind-blown scarfs, would trudge,
unspeaking, down to the forlorn sea, to work up
an appetite, to blow away the fumes,

Who knows, to walk into the waves
until nothing of them was left but
the two curling smoke clouds of
the inextinguishable briars.

Then I would be slap-dashing home, the gravy smell of the dinners of others, the bird smell, the brandy, the pudding and mince, coiling up to my nostrils, when out of a snow-clogged side lane would come a boy the spit of myself, with a pink-tipped cigarette and the violet past of a black eye, cocky as a bullfinch, leering all to himself.

hated him on sight and sound, and would
be about to put my dog whistle to my lips
and blow him off the face of Christmas when
suddenly he, with a violet wink, put *his* whistle
to *his* lips and blew so stridently, so high, so
exquisitely loud, that gobbling faces, their cheeks
bulged with goose, would press against their
tinselled windows, the whole length of the white
echoing street.

For dinner we had turkey and blazing pudding, and after dinner the Uncles sat in front of the fire, loosened all buttons, put their large moist hands over their watch chains, groaned a little and slept.

Mothers, aunts and sisters
scuttled to and fro, bearing tureens.
Auntie Bessie, who had already
been frightened, twice, by a clock-work mouse,
whimpered at the sideboard and had some
elderberry wine. The dog was sick. Auntie Dosie
had to have three aspirins, but Auntie Hannah,
who liked port, stood in the middle
of the snowbound back yard, singing like
a big-bosomed thrush.

I would blow up balloons to see how big they would blow up to; and, when they burst, which they all did, the Uncles jumped and rumbled. In the rich and heavy afternoon, the Uncles breathing like dolphins and the snow descending, I would sit among festoons and Chinese lanterns and nibble dates and try to make a model man-o'-war, following the Instructions for Little Engineers, and produce what might be mistaken for a sea-going tramcar.

Or I would go out, my bright new boots squeaking, into the white world, on to the seaward hill, to call on Jim and Dan and Jack and to pad through the still streets, leaving huge deep footprints on the hidden pavements.

'I bet people will think there's been hippos.'

'What would you do if you saw a hippo coming down our street?'

'I'd go like this, bang! I'd throw him over the railings and roll him down the hill and then I'd tickle him under the ear and he'd wag his tail.'

'What would you do if you saw *two* hippos?'

Iron-flanked and bellowing he-hippos clanked and battered through the scudding snow towards us as we passed Mr Daniel's house.

'Let's post Mr Daniel a snowball through his letter-box.'

'Let's write things in the snow.'

'Let's write, "Mr Daniel looks like a spaniel" all over his lawn.'

Or we walked on the white shore.

'Can the fishes see it's snowing?'

The silent one-clouded heavens drifted on to the sea. Now we were snow-blind travellers lost on the north hills, and vast dewlapped dogs, with flasks round their necks, ambled and shambled up to us, baying "Excelsior". We returned home through the poor streets where only a few children fumbled with bare red fingers in the wheel-rutted snow and cat-called after us, their voices fading away, as we trudged uphill, into the cries of the dock birds and the hooting of ships out in the whirling bay.

And then, at tea the recovered Uncles would be jolly; and the ice cake loomed in the centre of the table like a marble grave. Auntie Hannah laced her tea with rum, because it was only once a year.

Bring out the tall tales now that we told by the fire as the gaslight bubbled like a diver. Ghosts whooed like owls in the long nights when I dared not look over my shoulder; animals lurked in the cubbyhole under the stairs where the gas meter ticked.

And I remember that we went singing
carols once, when there wasn't the
shaving of a moon to light the flying streets.
At the end of a long road was a drive that led to
a large house, and we stumbled up the darkness
of the drive that night, each one of us afraid,
each one holding a stone in his hand in case,
and all of us too brave to say a word.

The wind through the trees made noises
as of old and unpleasant and maybe webfooted
men wheezing in caves. We reached the black
bulk of the house.

'What shall we give them?
Hark the Herald?'

'No,' Jack said, 'Good King Wenceslas.
I'll count three.'

One, two, three, and we began to sing,
our voices high and seemingly distant in
the snow-felted darkness round the house
that was occupied by nobody we knew.
We stood close together, near the dark door.

Good King Wenceslas looked out

On the Feast of Stephen . . .

And then a small, dry voice, like the voice of someone who has not spoken for a long time, joined our singing: a small, dry, eggshell voice from the other side of the door: a small dry voice through the keyhole. And when we stopped running we were outside *our* house; the front room was lovely; balloons floated under the hot-water-bottle-gulping gas; everything was good again and shone over the town.

'Perhaps it was a ghost,' Jim said.

'Perhaps it was trolls,' Dan said, who was always reading.

'Let's go in and see if there's any jelly left,' Jack said. And we did that.

Always on Christmas night there was music. An uncle played the fiddle, a cousin sang 'Cherry Ripe', and another uncle sang 'Drake's Drum'. It was very warm in the little house.

Auntie Hannah, who had got on to the parsnip wine, sang a song about Bleeding Hearts and Death, and then another in which she said her heart was like a Bird's Nest; and then everybody laughed again; and then I went to bed.

Looking through my bedroom window, out into the moonlight and the unending smoke-coloured snow, I could see the lights in the windows of all the other houses on our hill and hear the music rising from them up the long, steadily falling night. I turned the gas down, I got into bed. I said some words to the close and holy darkness, and then I slept.